Dear Parent:

Congratulations! Your child is taking the first steps on an exciting journey. The destination? Independent reading!

STEP INTO READING® will help your child get there. The program offers five steps to reading success. Each step includes fun stories and colorful art. There are also Step into Reading Sticker Books, Step into Reading Math Readers, Step into Reading Write-In Readers, Step into Reading Phonics Readers, and Step into Reading Phonics First Steps! Boxed Sets—a complete literacy program with something for every child.

Learning to Read, Step by Step!

Ready to Read Preschool–Kindergarten
• big type and easy words • rhyme and rhythm • picture clues
For children who know the alphabet and are eager to begin reading.

Reading with Help Preschool–Grade 1
• basic vocabulary • short sentences • simple stories
For children who recognize familiar words and sound out new words with help.

Reading on Your Own Grades 1–3
• engaging characters • easy-to-follow plots • popular topics
For children who are ready to read on their own.

Reading Paragraphs Grades 2–3
• challenging vocabulary • short paragraphs • exciting stories
For newly independent readers who read simple sentences with confidence.

Ready for Chapters Grades 2–4
• chapters • longer paragraphs • full-color art
For children who want to take the plunge into chapter books but still like colorful pictures.

STEP INTO READING® is designed to give every child a successful reading experience. The grade levels are only guides. Children can progress through the steps at their own speed, developing confidence in their reading, no matter what their grade.

Remember, a lifetime love of reading starts with a single step!

To Patti and Chris Kirigan
—J.C.

For Dan—L.M.

Text copyright © 1987 by Joanna Cole.
Illustrations copyright © 1987 by Lynn Munsinger.
All rights reserved under International and Pan-American Copyright Conventions. Published in the United States by Random House Children's Books, a division of Random House, Inc., New York, and simultaneously in Canada by Random House of Canada Limited, Toronto.

www.stepintoreading.com

Educators and librarians, for a variety of teaching tools, visit us at
www.randomhouse.com/teachers

Library of Congress Cataloging-in-Publication Data
Cole, Joanna.
Norma Jean, jumping bean / by Joanna Cole ; illustrated by Lynn Munsinger.
   p.   cm. — (Step into reading. A step 3 book)
SUMMARY: Norma Jean, whose love of jumping might be a bit excessive, stops her favorite activity after her friends complain, but participation in the school Olympics proves there is a time and place for jumping.
ISBN 0-394-88668-2 (trade) — ISBN 0-394-98668-7 (lib. bdg.)
[1. Jumping—Fiction. 2. Kangaroos—Fiction. 3. Animals—Fiction.]
I. Munsinger, Lynn, ill.   II. Title.   III. Series: Step into reading. Step 3 book.
PZ7.C67346   No 2003   [E]— dc21   2002013657

Printed in the United States of America   51 50 49 48 47 46

STEP INTO READING, RANDOM HOUSE, and the Random House colophon are registered trademarks of Random House, Inc.

STEP INTO READING®

STEP 3

Norma Jean, Jumping Bean

by Joanna Cole

illustrated by Lynn Munsinger

Random House 🏠 New York

Norma Jean liked to jump.

In the morning

she jumped out of bed.

She jumped

into her clothes.

She jumped

down the stairs.

Norma Jean jumped

all the way to school.

She jumped past

Amy, Sam,

Nell, and Ted.

"Wow!" said Ted.

"Look at her go!

That Norma Jean

never stops jumping!"

"Hello hello hello!"

she called to her friends.

That morning

Miss Jones read a book

to the class.

It was a very good book.

But Norma Jean did not

sit still long enough

to hear the story.

At playtime

Norma Jean and Nell

built a tower of blocks.

Norma Jean was so excited.

She jumped up and down.

Oh, no!

No more tower.

At lunch

Sam gave Norma Jean

a cupcake.

Norma Jean was so happy.

She jumped up and down.

Oh, no!

Her milk spilled

all over Sam.

"Norma Jean,

please sit still,"

said Miss Jones.

"This is not the time

or place for jumping."

After school

Norma Jean went

to visit Ted.

"Hello hello hello!"

she shouted to Ted.

"Will you play with me?"

"Okay," said Ted.

"Let's get on my seesaw."

But Norma Jean bounced too hard.

Ted almost flew off the seesaw.

"I don't want to play anymore,"
Ted said.
"I wonder why Ted
is mad at me,"
said Norma Jean.

Then she jumped over to Amy's house.

Amy was playing in her pool.

"Hello hello hello!"

said Norma Jean.

"May I play too?"

Amy said, "Sure.

Jump in!"

That was the wrong thing
to say to Norma Jean!
SPLASH!

Amy got out of the pool.

"Why did you get out?"

asked Norma Jean.

"We are having so much fun!"

Amy said,

"You are having fun.

I am going inside.

It is no fun playing

with a jumping bean!"

Now Norma Jean knew why
her friends were mad at her.

The next day

Norma Jean walked

to school very slowly.

There was a big puddle.

All the other kids

jumped over it.

But Norma Jean did not jump.

Norma Jean said,

"I don't want to be a jumping bean.

No more jumping for Norma Jean."

So she walked

through the puddle

and got her feet all wet.

In the school yard

kids were running around

and playing catch

and jumping rope.

"There's Norma Jean,"
said Amy.
"Come jump with us."
But Norma Jean
said no.

Norma Jean said,

"I don't want to be a jumping bean.

No more jumping for Norma Jean."

And she just stood there

and watched the other kids jump rope.

At the end of the day

Miss Jones told the class

that Field Day was coming soon.

There were going to be

lots of races.

Ted wanted to be

in the egg-and-spoon race.

Amy and Sam

said they would be

in the wheelbarrow race.

Nell asked if she could be

in the rope-climbing contest.

FIELD DAY
EGG + SPOON RACE
   TED
WHEELBARROW RACE
   SAM + AMY
ROPE CLIMBING
   NELL
JUMPING CONTESTS

"Now, who will be in

the jumping contests?"

asked Miss Jones.

Everybody shouted,

"Norma Jean! Norma Jean!

She is the best jumper in school!"

34

But Norma Jean said,

"I don't want to be a jumping bean.

No more jumping for Norma Jean."

Ted said,

"I miss the old Norma Jean.

She was fun,

even if she did jump a lot."

On Field Day,

Ted won

the egg-and-spoon race.

Norma Jean was very happy.

She yelled,

"Hooray! Hooray!"

Amy and Sam

came in first

in the wheelbarrow race.

Norma Jean yelled,

"Hooray hooray hooray!"

And she jumped up and down

just a little bit.

Nell won

the rope-climbing contest.

Norma Jean was so excited,
she jumped out
on the field.

Norma Jean was
just in time for
the hurdles,

the high jump,

and the potato-sack race.

She won them all.

"Hooray hooray hooray!"

shouted the kids in Miss Jones's class.

Norma Jean was very happy.

But she did not jump up and down.

She stood very still.

Miss Jones pinned

a blue ribbon

on Norma Jean.

It said,

"Norma Jean, Champion Jumping Bean."

What did Norma Jean do then?

Norma Jean jumped for joy.

She jumped

and she jumped

and she jumped

all the way home.

After all,

there <u>is</u> a time

and a place

for jumping.